U-SHAPED SHOES

By Melba Collazo Ellmore

Illustrated by Susan Roseberry

Ideals Children's Books • Nashville, Tennessee
an imprint of Hambleton-Hill Publishing, Inc.

For Mom and Dad, and for Bill

—*M. C. E.*

Dedicated to my husband, Tim, and my children, Matthew and Jennifer.
—*S. R.*

Published by Ideals Children's Books
An imprint of Hambleton-Hill Publishing, Inc.
Nashville, Tennessee 37218

Printed and bound in Mexico

Library of Congress Cataloging-in-Publication Data
Ellmore, Melba C.
    U-Shaped Shoes / by Melba C. Ellmore ; illustrated by Susan Roseberry. —
1st ed.
        p.   cm. —
    Summary: After searching for his missing shoes among the barnyard
animals, Sam the horse not only recovers the lost objects but also learns a new
game that can be played with them.
    ISBN 1-57102-116-7 (hc)
    [1. Shoes—Fiction. 2. Lost and found possessions—Fiction. 3. Horses—
Fiction. 4. Domestic animals—Fiction. 5. Stories in rhyme.] I. Roseberry,
Susan, ill. II. Title.
    PZ8.3.E4965Us   1998
    [E]—DC21   97-6153
                                                    CIP
                                                    AC

The illustrations in this book were rendered in colored pencil on Bristol board.
The text type was set in Sabon Regular.
The display type was set in Old Town No 536 D Ro 1.

First Edition

10 9 8 7 6 5 4 3 2 1

Sam,

the nicest horse you'd ever meet,

sat staring at his naked feet.

He scratched his head, a bit confused.

It seemed he'd lost two pairs of shoes!

Not one, not two, not three, but four!

What a problem! What a chore

to try to think where they might be,

those shoes he'd worn since he was three.

They could be here or near or there.

They could be almost anywhere.

And then he thought, *For goodness' sake,*
did someone take them by mistake?
Sam was new there to the farm;
he looked around with some alarm.
Who might have his pairs of shoes?

He then began to look for clues.
He trotted off at barefoot speed
and came across some chicken feed.
He followed close this seedy trail;
it led him to a hidden bale.

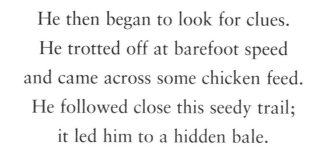

Behind it three hens sat and played
a lively game of hen Old Maid.
They talked. They squawked. They drank their tea.
Sam watched and waited patiently.
And then he asked them if they knew
where he might find his U-shaped shoes.
"Oh my," they clucked, "that old style?
We've not seen that for quite a while."

He saw then when he looked below
high-heeled pumps with little bows!
High-heeled shoes on a hen!
He blinked his eyes and looked again.
These were not the kind he wore.
"Good-bye," he said. "I'll search some more."

He heard some snorts behind the shed.
"I've heard that sound before," Sam said.
And over by the flower mound,
four marble-playing pigs he found.

"I don't know if perhaps today,"
he asked them as he watched them play,
"you might have seen some shoes my size?"

They looked at him with mild surprise.
"We only wear this type, you know.
We don't like shoes that pinch our toes."
Sam quickly saw the pigs weren't wrong
for on their feet were *bright pink thongs!*
Imagine that! Those silly guys
wearing thongs, piggy size!

"My shoes aren't here, I have a hunch,"
Sam sighed and left the noisy bunch.

"Where are my shoes? It makes no sense,"
he muttered as he reached the fence.
And on the fence, two solemn sheep
were playing chess without a peep.

They played their game quite long and slow.
Sam finally said, "I've got to know
if you have seen some shoes, two pair,
the kind of shoes that horses wear?"

They didn't look, just answered back,
"The kind we wear are white and black."
And neatly crossed below their seats
were *saddle oxfords on their feet!*

Sam stood there thinking, quite perplexed.
He shook his head, "What will come next?"
And why was it so hard to find,
his pairs of shoes, the U-shaped kind?
He told the sheep, "I've got to go.
Where I'll look next, I just don't know."

And then he heard some shouts and yells.
Behind the barn? He couldn't tell.
He peeked behind the big, red wall
and saw a game of goat kickball!

Sam asked a goat (she looked quite sweet),
"Have you seen 'U's that fit my feet?"

"Our games," she said, "are often rough.
We wear shoes that are strong and tough."
She kicked the ball and made it soar.
That's when he saw the *boots* she wore!

The goat ran up to second base.
Sam left to look some other place.

He heard a bunch of giggling cows,
and asked himself, "Oh no! What now?"
He saw them as they ran and peeked.
The game they played was hide-and-seek.

He said, "Excuse and pardon me—
do you know where my shoes might be?"
They smiled and swayed on lifted toes
and whispered back, "We just don't know."
Then off they pranced with gentle moos
in lovely cow-sized *ballet shoes!*

Sam was left quite all alone.
He blinked back tears, let out a moan.
"I'll walk," he said with trembling chin,
"with naked feet from here on in.
Those old four shoes, the shoes I wore,
are gone for good. I'll search no more."
And as he shed a big horse tear,
a little crowd gathered near—
a crowd of cows, goats, sheep, pigs, hens;
Sam did not know they were his friends.

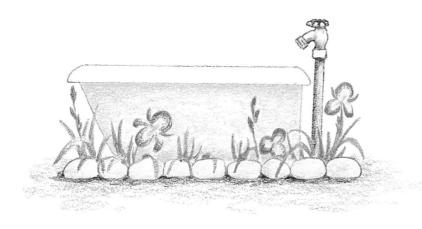

Two other horses came near too.
They said, "We have a gift for you."
A box they gave, wrapped with care;
his four lost shoes were tucked in there.
And underneath, to his surprise,
were high-top shoes, just his size!

"Your shoes weren't right," the horses said.
"We got a different kind instead.
To get your size, just to be sure,
we measured those old shoes you wore.
Since you're like us, big and tall,
you might enjoy horse basketball!"

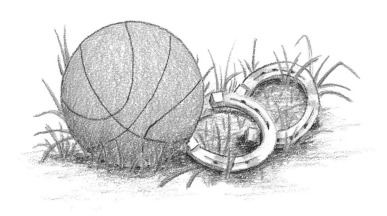

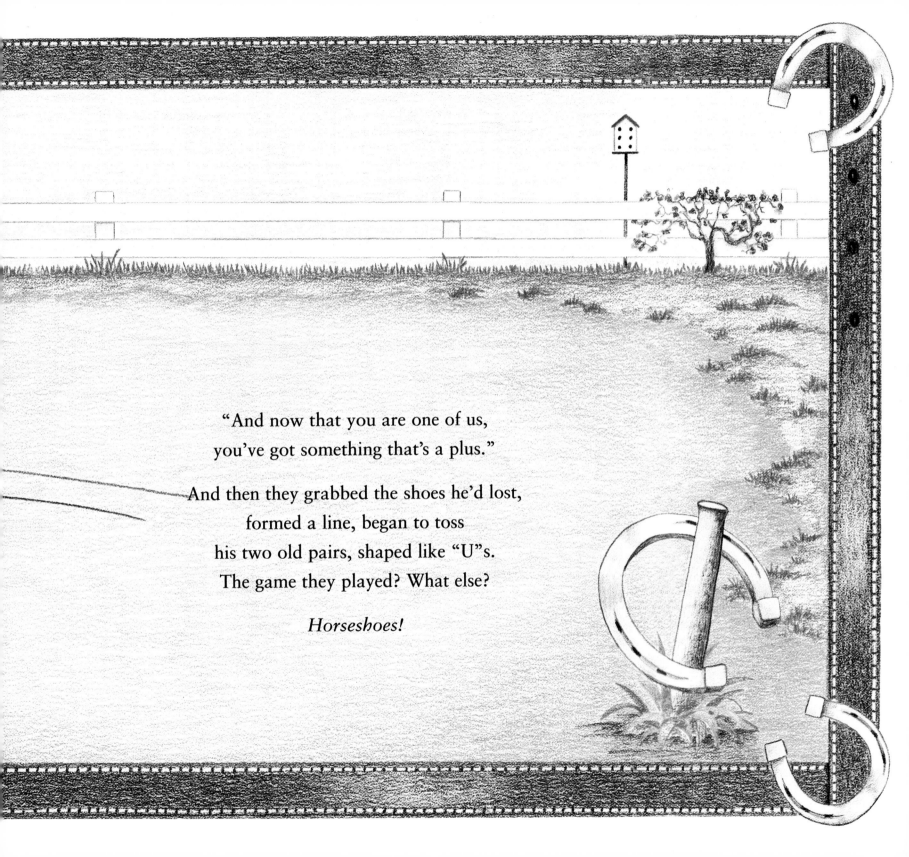

"And now that you are one of us,
you've got something that's a plus."

And then they grabbed the shoes he'd lost,
formed a line, began to toss
his two old pairs, shaped like "U"s.
The game they played? What else?

Horseshoes!